ideals EASTER

D0534335

Vol. 47, No. 2

Publisher, Patricia A. Pingry
Editor, Cynthia Wyatt
Art Director, Patrick McRae
Production Manager, Jeff Wyatt
Editorial Assistant, Kathleen Gilbert
Copy Editors, Marian Hollyday
          Nancy Skarmeas
          Robin Crouch

ISBN 0-8249-1081-8

IDEALS—Vol. 47, No. 2 March MCMXC IDEALS (ISSN 0019-137X) is published eight times a year: February, March, May, June, August, September, November, December by IDEALS PUBLISHING CORPORATION, Nelson Place at Elm Hill Pike, Nashville, Tenn. 37214. Second-class postage paid at Nashville, Tennessee, and additional mailing offices. Copyright © MCMXC by IDEALS PUBLISHING CORPORATION. POSTMASTER: Send address changes to Ideals, Post Office Box 148000, Nashville, Tenn. 37214-8000. All rights reserved. Title IDEALS registered U.S. Patent Office.

SINGLE ISSUE—$4.95
ONE-YEAR SUBSCRIPTION—eight consecutive issues as published—$19.95
TWO-YEAR SUBSCRIPTION—sixteen consecutive issues as published—$35.95
Outside U.S.A., add $6.00 per subscription year for postage and handling.

ACKNOWLEDGEMENTS

A PRAYER IN SPRING from *THE POETRY OF ROBERT FROST* edited by Edward Connery Lathem. Copyright 1934, © 1969 by Holt, Rinehart and Winston. Copyright 1962 by Robert Frost. Reprinted by arrangement with Henry Holt and Company, Inc.; THE WIDE OUTDOORS from *WHEN DAY IS DONE* by Edgar A. Guest. Copyright 1921 by The Reilly & Lee co. Reprinted by permission of the Estate; A PRAYER FOR DAWN from *THE HEART CONTENT* by Douglas Malloch. Copyright 1926, 1927 by Douglas Malloch. Reprinted by permission of the Estate; RIGHT WHERE YOU ARE from *MOMENTS OF SUNSHINE* by Garnett Ann Schultz. Copyright © 1974 by Garnett Ann Schultz. Reprinted by permission. Our sincere thanks to the following whose addresses we were unable to locate: Arthur L. Fischer for ALL IN HIS GOOD TIME; the estate of Elizabeth Lathrop Powers for SPRING'S REBIRTH from *RYTHM ROAD*, Copyright 1951.

Four-color separations by Rayson Films, Inc., Waukesha, Wisconsin

Printing by Ringier-America, Brookfield, Wisconsin

The paper used in this publication meets the minimum requirements of American National Standard for Information Sciences—Permanence of Paper for Printed Library Materials, ANSI Z39.48-1984.

Cover
Lisse, Holland
Manfred Thonig/H. Armstrong Roberts

VILLAGE SPRINGTIME
Donald Mills

SPRING'S REBIRTH

Elizabeth Lathrop Powers

Springtime—and earth awakens,
Nature clothes herself anew;
After winter's bleakness
Spring comes smiling through.

Springtime—and tender grass
Spreads softly, greenly, o'er the lawn,
While chirping robins cheerfully
Proclaim the early dawn.

Springtime brings the sunshine—
Beams that warmly penetrate
To the darkly hidden spots
Where the germs of life await.

Springtime means new beginnings,
Sermons in each tender shoot;
Peach and plum and apple blossoms
Promise give of summer fruit.

Springtime—and Easter's message—
Earth adopts a hopeful mood.
Easter means resurrection,
Life and strength and faith renewed.

Easter—and reassurance
Soothes a weary, ravaged earth;
As again her people witness
The changeless miracle of spring's rebirth.

Photo Opposite
BIRDHOUSE IN SPRING
Fred Sieb Photography

TO A DANDELION

Mary Frances Phillips

A golden-headed beauty nodding in the morning sun.
A lovely ball of silver when the golden orb is done.
A hollow leg to stand on in palest shade of green.
Born in early spring and nestled in a salad green.
A gift from children to their mothers to grace a special place
Reserved for extra-nice bouquets in the very nicest vase.

"Do you like butter?" a child asks and picks a flowerlet or two,
So sure of finding out by simply testing it on you.
Compliantly you go along and play the game anew,
Expressing your desire to know the helpful answer too.
Held beneath the lifted chin to test with its caress—
If its gold's reflected on you, 'tis proof that it is "yes."

The seeded silver threads when gently blown on dance away
And gaily go a-sailing off upon a summer's day.
Split the hollow stem end and curl it back just so,
Dip in soapy water and prismatic bubbles blow.
Nature's handy bubble pipe, a thrill to laughing tots
Who blow a million bubbles to soar a time, then pop.

"A common weed" some people sigh while rooting it away.
But if dandelions were rarities, perchance they'd seek a way
To find some silver-threaded seeds to nurture with great care;
Each bloom would be a treasure. They'd braid them for their hair,
Take pleasure in a steaming brew of dandelion tea,
And snip the leaves for salad—how devoted they would be.

Photo Opposite
DANDELIONS
H. Thonig/H. Armstrong Roberts

ALL IN HIS GOOD TIME

Arthur L. Fischer

When the weather's eccentricities
At last have had their fling
With people longing hopefully
For a sight of settled spring;
When rain-filled clouds leave grudgingly
And the sun bursts out to shine,
Brightening the tulips,
Forcing fragrance from the pine;
And meadowlarks sing sweetly
As they circle through the skies
Of the God-created beauty
That lies spread before their eyes;
Then I add my timid tenor
To their hymn of thankful praise
While wondering at the strangeness
And wisdom of His ways!

Photo Overleaf
CASCADING BLOSSOMS
BELLEVILLE, NEW JERSEY
Gene Ahrens/H. Armstrong Roberts

Photo Opposite
MUNSON FALLS
MANCHESTER VILLAGE, VERMONT
Dick Smith Photography

Gratitude

Beverly J. Anderson

We thank You, God, for beauty
That comes with each new spring:
The greening hills and valleys,
The songbirds on the wing,
The meadow flowers waking
And waltzing in the breeze,
Bright sunbeams gaily dancing
Upon the new-leafed trees.

FALSE RUE ANEMONE
Adam Jones

The jonquils in their bonnets
With trim of beaded dew,
The tulip cups unfolding
In shades of brilliant hue,
The pink-white apple blossoms
Against the soft blue sky,
The fluffy clouds and sunshine,
The mountains towering high,

The rainbow-tinted colors
Aglow across the land—
For such a wealth of splendor
Created by Your hand.
In gratitude, our Father,
We lift our hearts in praise,
Rejoicing in Your blessings
Throughout the springtime days.

MOURNING DOVES IN DOGWOOD
Adam Jones

11

A Prayer in Spring

Robert Frost

Oh, give us pleasure in the flowers today;
And give us not to think so far away
As the uncertain harvest; keep us here
All simply in the springing of the year.

Oh, give us pleasure in the orchard white,
Like nothing else by day, like ghosts by night;
And make us happy in the happy bees,
The swarm dilating round the perfect trees.

And make us happy in the darting bird
That suddenly above the bees is heard,
The meteor that thrusts in with needle bill,
And off a blossom in midair stands still.

For this is love and nothing else is love,
The which it is reserved for God above
To sanctify to what far ends He will,
But which it only needs that we fulfill.

Photo Overleaf
PARK NEAR LISSE
HOLLAND
M. Thonig/H. Armstrong Roberts

Photo Opposite
FLOWERING CHERRY
JOSEPHINE GARDENS
WILMINGTON, VIRGINIA
Gottlieb Hampfler

Meringue Confections

Meringue Shells
Makes 6 shells

3 egg whites
1/4 teaspoon cream of tartar
1/8 teaspoon salt
3/4 cup granulated sugar

Preheat oven to 275°. Beat egg whites until foamy; add cream of tartar and salt; beat until stiff but not dry. Gradually add sugar, beating until very stiff. Cover baking sheet with heavy brown paper or aluminum foil. Shape meringue, with spoon or pastry bag, into 6 rounds about 3 inches in diameter on baking sheet. Make a 2-inch diameter depression in center of each. Bake 1 hour. Cool.

Orange Swirls
Makes 6 servings

3 egg yolks
2 tablespoons granulated sugar
1/8 teaspoon salt
6 tablespoons frozen orange concentrate, thawed and undiluted
1 1/2 teaspoons grated orange rind
1 cup heavy cream, whipped
6 orange sections
6 meringue shells

Beat egg yolks in top of double boiler. Add sugar, salt and orange juice concentrate. Cook over boiling water, stirring constantly, until thickened. Remove from heat; add orange rind and chill. Fold in whipped cream. Spoon into meringue shells. Chill 12 to 14 hours. Garnish with orange sections.

Fresh Fruit Parfaits
Makes 6 servings

1 1/2 cups sour cream
1 1/2 tablespoons grated orange peel
1 1/2 tablespoons honey
1 1/2 tablespoons brown sugar
2 oranges, peeled and cut into bite-size pieces
2 bananas, sliced
3/4 cup canned pineapple chunks, drained
6 meringue shells

In a small bowl combine sour cream, orange peel, honey, and brown sugar. Layer fruit with sour cream mixture in meringue shells. Chill before serving.

Ice Cream with Berry Topping
Makes 6 servings

1 can (16 to 17 ounces) blackberries, boysenberries, marionberries, blueberries, or raspberries
1 tablespoon cornstarch
1 of the following flavorings:
1 tablespoon lemon juice;
1/2 teaspoon lemon juice;
1/2 teaspoon grated lemon or orange peel
1 to 2 tablespoon butter, optional
6 meringue shells

Drain berries; reserve syrup. In a small saucepan combine reserved syrup and cornstarch; stir to dissolve cornstarch. Cook and stir until thickened. Add desired flavoring and butter (optional). Gently stir in berries. Chill. Fill meringue shells with ice cream and cover with fruit topping.

Photo Opposite
ORANGE SWIRLS

The Great Masterpiece

Jean Frances Zyats

The sleeping Earth wakens,
God's summons obeys,
Bids her latent treasures—
Behold the new day!

All buds in your cradles
Rocked to and fro;
And blossoms unborn yet,
Asleep under snow;

All branches—break forth now!
Fair creatures to hide.
With resplendence grace
The wan countryside.

All ye sleeping creatures,
Your wintry rest cease.
Awake! Take your place in
The great Masterpiece.

An Easter Wish

June Masters Bacher

The world springs up
All fresh and sweet,
With wings of faith
Upon its feet . . .

Would that each heart
Were more like it:
By hope made strong
And faith made fit

To reach toward God's
Eternal blue
With love that polishes
It like new—

A heart that hopes
And prays and sings
And soars by faith
On Easter wings.

BUNNY NESTS

Dan A. Hoover

On Easter Eve when we were small
And evening mist began to fall,
A time we little ones loved best
Was the building of our Bunny Nests.

Mom had some little baskets made
So we filled these with straw;
We hid them here and there and hoped
The Easter Bunny saw.

It was so hard to wait that night,
We hardly slept at all,
And kept Old Spot inside in case
Our long-eared friend should call.

Next morning it was hardly light,
We flew outside to see;
And sure enough, he'd passed that way
With gifts for Sis and me.

Marshmallow eggs and candy eggs
With real eggs brown as toffee—
Just like the ones we saw last night
Which Mom had boiled in coffee!

Dad grinned mysteriously and said
You couldn't always tell
What that old rascal sometimes did.
Had we looked by the well?

There must have been two dozen there,
Like rainbows to our eyes.
Both Mom and Dad were smiling,
Enjoying our surprise.

Long years have passed, yet every spring
When Eastertime appears,
I see our little Bunny Nests,
Sometimes through mists of tears.

Photo Opposite
EASTER EGGS AND HYACINTHS
Ina Mackey

SPRING JOURNEY

Ruth B. Field

In the springtime we hitched up good old Nell
And Gram and I rode away to town
With a *clip-clop* through the sweet spring smell
To buy a new hat and maybe a gown

With a guimpe and a sash; and some squeaky shoes.
Like tassels the catkins hung in the sun.
In town we would hear the latest news
And visit the notion store—what fun!

Penny dolls, candy in jars, bright beads,
Mustache cups, calico, crockery ware—
Here we could satisfy all our needs—
Ah, lovely the time that we spent there.

Burnished with joy were those sunny hours
Spent on a happy springtime ride—
Ring on a candy stick and flowers
On a hat as bright as the countryside.

Back over the road when the sun went down,
With precious bundles—life was a sonnet
To spring and a buggy ride to town
And a dream come true, my beflowered bonnet.

Easter Bonnets in Waiting

Harriette M. Hinz

I've made careful observations
And won't be overstating
To disclose milady's closets hold
Much-loved "chapeaus-in-waiting!"

We plucked them from our bouffant curls,
Tucked them safely away
When fashion deemed that Easter hats
Must take a holiday!

Soft tissue folds hold bright, crisp straws
'Twixt ribbons by the yard.
Boxed posies bloom in eagerness
To stroll the boulevard!

When March defers to April, then
We'll peek 'neath lids once more
But wait for fickle fashion
To declare a hat encore!

Photo Opposite
FANCY-DRESS BONNETS
Gerald Koser

Clara Barton,
the Angel of the Battlefield

On Christmas Day in 1821, America received a wonderful Christmas present: the birth of a baby girl named Clarissa Harlowe Barton. It would be years before the nation realized the value of this new life, the fifth child of charitable, hardworking parents in North Oxford, Massachusetts. But before her death in 1912 this quiet, intelligent woman would found the American Red Cross and spread the merciful balm of medical and relief supplies to American soldiers and civilians suffering the ravages of war and catastrophic weather.

Her family background instilled in her the value of good works. Her parents, Captain Stephen Barton and Sara Stone Barton, were devout Christians. The Captain contributed regularly to the county poor fund and used his money to establish a house for destitute families. Sara Stone Barton was an energetic and productive mother and housewife whose vitality must have affected little Clara, because she could read and write when she entered school at the age of four.

Clara grew up to establish a reputation as an outstanding teacher in the county's public school system.

In 1854, after ten years of teaching in Massachusetts, Clara moved to Washington, D.C., and became the first woman clerk in the U.S. Patent Office. The onslaught of the Civil War when she was forty was the turning point in her life.

The Twenty-first Massachusetts was among the scores of regiments reporting to Washington after the fall of Fort Sumter. Clara recognized former pupils, now adults, and became involved in caring for them. She brought food and supplies to those who were quartered in the U.S. Senate chamber and read them their hometown newspapers. It was the beginning of her lifelong commitment to the victims of war, and later, to victims of natural catastrophe.

After the first battle of Manassas, Clara Barton was appalled at the lack of Army medical supplies. She began soliciting support from citizens and eventually filled three warehouses with bandages, medical supplies, and blankets.

Distributing her supplies to the front sometimes became as difficult as collecting them. While Union generals called her work "meddlesome," medical personnel felt otherwise. After the battle at Cedar Mountain, she arrived at a field hospital at midnight with supplies. One of the surgeons there wrote, "I thought that night if heaven ever sent out a holy angel, she must be the one, her assistance was so timely." Thereafter she was known as "the Angel of the Battlefield."

Clara's bravery silenced her detractors. At Fredericksburg, as a Union officer was assisting her across a pontoon bridge, an exploding shell tore away a portion of her skirt and his coattail. And at Antietam, while she was attempting to aid a wounded soldier, a bullet passed through her clothing. It killed the young man in her arms.

After the war, President Lincoln appointed her to assist in locating missing prisoners of war. She undertook this task until 1869 when her failing health required that she rest in Europe. Thus began another great phase in her life.

It was in Geneva that she met Jean-Henri Dunart, founder of the International Red Cross. She learned about the organization and its work, joined as a volunteer, and assumed the role of battlefield nurse during the Franco-Prussian war.

She returned to the United States determined to help ratify the Geneva Convention, an agreement regarding the treatment of enemy wounded and prisoners of war, which gave the Red Cross neutrality on the battlefields of Europe. She found little support in Washington because government officials feared "foreign entanglements." She lobbied Congress, met with three presidents, and her efforts finally paid off when Chester A. Arthur signed the treaty on March 1, 1882. The Senate concurred and the U.S. became the thirty-second nation to join the International Red Cross.

In the following years, Clara Barton created a new role for the American Red Cross. While the international organization concentrated its efforts on military conflicts, Clara saw an important function for the Red Cross during peacetime. She felt it should provide aid and assistance during natural disasters and traveled extensively to prove her point. Under the Red Cross flag she organized relief efforts for victims of Michigan forest fires; chartered steamers to take supplies down the Ohio and Mississippi rivers to help flooded families; and spearheaded the work to aid victims of the Johnstown flood.

After the war Congress named the Red Cross the official relief agency for civilian and military personnel. Clara Barton's final field work before retiring was organizing aid to hurricane victims at Galveston, Texas, in 1900. She died in her Glen Echo, Maryland, home in 1912.

How did such a shy, quiet person accomplish so much? Clara explains much when she writes in her diary her father's advice to her as she cared for him during his long, terminal illness:

"As a patriot, he bade me serve my country with all I had, even my life if need be; as a daughter of an accepted Mason, he bade me seek and comfort the afflicted everywhere; and as a Christian, he charged me to honor God and love mankind."

Wallace Sears

Wallace Sears works in public relations. His articles and short stories have appeared in the Christian Science Monitor *and other publications. He lives with his family in Kissimmee, Florida.*

COLLECTOR'S CORNER

Hatpins

Three hatpins in Art Deco geometric designs, circa 1920— Egyptian designs were popularized with the discovery of the "Valley of the Kings" burial sites during this period.

When women dressed for Easter in the late ninteenth and early twentieth century, they held their Easter bonnets in place with a hatpin, and in doing so, were enjoying one of the fruits of the industrial era of mass production. The history of hatpins and pins in general has attracted collectors with the story it tells about society's dress habits and the gradual liberation of women!

Pins are a much taken for granted, functional item in our wardrobe today, but before the invention of the pin-making machine, pins were treasured as handcrafted luxuries essential to the elaborate ruffles and folds of upper-class wardrobes only dreamed about by the peasants who had to lace their clothing closed. It took seven men to make a single pin, and stealing a handmade pin was a crime punishable by hanging! In England, the Queen's pins were paid for with taxes collected on the first day of the New Year. It was on this day only that her subjects were permitted to purchase pins of their own, thus originating the expression, "pin money."

When hatpins were produced in mass quantities by machine, they became more affordable, and a widespread rise in hatpin popularity resulted. Coincidentally, the manufacture of artificial flowers was perfected and increased the popularity of hats. Dressmakers and milliners rose to the challenge, using their imagination and creativity to adorn hats with a wide array of flowers and embellishments. Hatpins manufactured from 1850 to 1925 are the collectible "period" hatpins. During that time women's hairstyles were often quite elaborate. Cotton batting, wires, and false hair were added to augment the volume of the hairstyle. Throughout this period lavish hats of unsurpassed perfection and creativity were made. These hats required numerous hatpins which became the finest examples of workmanship and are most prized by collectors today.

Unfortunately, along with the use of hatpins came problems, both social and legal. The hatpin began to be viewed as a potential danger. With hatpins sometimes reaching a length of twelve or more inches, people in streetcars and crowded places learned to avoid the protruding points. One postcard from 1910 shows a woman wearing a large hat with several long hatpins. Two of the sharp points are dangerously close to the face of the man with whom she is walking. The verse reads:

> "Excuse Me!" said the maiden hid
> Beneath Dame Fashion's latest lid.
> "I dearly love your eyes so blue.
> In fact, I'm really stuck on you."

In 1910 there was a furor over these "lethal weapons," and laws were passed to govern how long hatpins could be and how they could be worn in public. Some of these laws still remain on the books today. Later on, "guards" or "nibs" were designed to cover the exposed points.

Collectors differentiate between hatpin and hat pin (two words). A hat pin is a decorative pin that men use on their hats. More recently, it refers to the insignia on hats worn by both men and women in the armed forces. A hatpin is the pin women use to fasten their hats to their hair.

Hatpins were classified with jewelry and were listed as such in catalogs and brochures. Gift sets were popular and often included a pair of hatpins, collar buttons, blouse studs, and belt buckles with matching designs, as well as veil pins. The 1903 Sears and Roebuck catalog featured more than a dozen assorted hatpins. Unfortunately for the hatpin collector, many of the most valuable hatpins were converted into other pieces of jewelry before their value as a collectible was recognized.

Hand-carved Ivory Elephant atop ball, circa 1895

Many hatpin setting designs were borrowed from the art style of the past. Romanesque, Gothic, and Renaissance were the most preferred and were the main sources for the hatpin art of the Victorian, Edwardian, and Art Nouveau periods. Some of the most beautiful and sought-after hatpin designs were copied from antique jewelry.

Along with the popularity of the hatpin came many clever designs for hatpin holders. Most were designed like small porcelain vases or metal stands, and bisque figurines cast as hatpin bearers were also popular. The variety of design and craftsmanship of hatpin holders is as broad as that of the hatpins themselves and worthy of a closer look.

Hatpins represent an important part of histo-ry, and women's history in particular. Noted hatpin collector and author Lillian Baker writes that it is "the hatpin, of course, that enable[d] women to discard the bonnet strings and adopt the masculine attire—a hat—as their symbol of equality," in her definitive book on the subject, *Hatpins and Hatpin Holders, An Illustrated Value Guide.*

Ms. Baker sums it up well when she writes: "Hatpins and their related accessories are not only collectible but are legitimately part of our literature, the theatre, our folklore, and our politics."

Learning about hatpins and collecting them can be truly satisfying. With fashion's unpredictable trends, hatpins may one day resurface with their rich and interesting history and once again become a part of the Easter bonnet tradition.

Carol Shaw Johnston

Carol Shaw Johnston, a public school teacher, writes articles and short stories. She lives with her family in Nashville, Tennessee.

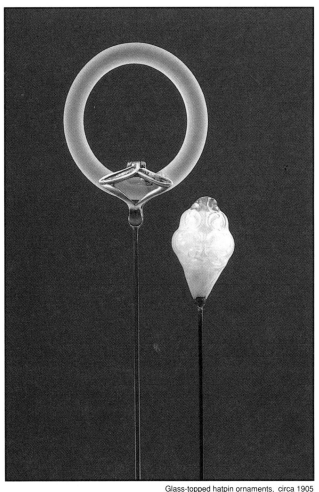

Glass-topped hatpin ornaments, circa 1905

Photography courtesy of Lillian Baker

In war as in peace, the art treasures of France are first in the public mind. The most precious of these in the various museums are being moved to bombproof shelters. Here an empty truck enters the Louvre for a load of masterpieces of art.

How French Have Insulated
Art Treasures Against War

The French Government's extensive efforts to protect its art treasures against air raids and other wartime disasters were outlined in a report made public by the Ministry of Education last week. Some side lights on French precautions:

In a sense, this war began in the Hall of Mirrors at Versailles in 1919—just as the last war sprang from another Versailles "peace" in 1871. Should a total war ever occur, Germany might logically try to wipe the scene of her World War humiliation off the map. So the furniture and portable treasures of the Sun King's great palace have been sent away for safekeeping; the Hall of Mirrors is banked with sandbags; the balcony where Marie Antoinette may have said "Let them eat cake" is boarded up; and the park is dotted with anti-aircraft stations.

During the Spanish war paintings from the Prado in Madrid were nearly ruined by mildew when they were stored in the damp vaults of the Bank of Spain (NEWSWEEK, July 17, 1939). So only jewels, glass, and similar objects have been stored under the solid stone-arch vaults of the Bank of France. Theatrical scenery movers used more than 250 trucks to cart the Louvre's 4,500 pictures to Châteaux in Southern France, where the humidity is slight. On this trek a gang of telephone repairmen cut and repaired telephone wires which obstructed free passage of pictures along the road.

Though stripped of pictures, the Louvre isn't empty. The School of Beaux Arts operates in one wing. Many of the 200 students (normal registration: 1,500), who are mostly women, sleep in the old palace, which is being redecorated inside—a much postponed job made possible by the evacuation. And in the Louvre's cellars, the Venus de Milo and the Winged Victory of Samothrace are suspended on ropes inside packing cases which are buried with sandbags.

In the Champ-de-Mars, soldiers guard the four sprawling legs of the Eiffel Tower, which houses radio, wireless, and television apparatus. This landmark, including the fashionable restaurant on top, is closed to the public.

Liquid fire no longer blazes in the windows of Sainte-Chapelle, Notre Dame, Chartres, and other cathedrals. Without shattering even one irreplacable fragment, workmen in the first three weeks of the war gingerly dismantled and packed more than 170,000 square feet of stained glass, which has been replaced with ordinary white glass. One result: the fluted columns and soaring Gothic masonry inside these world-famous churches are now visible as never before in their history.

Again as during the last war the French Government has (despite official denials) turned art critic. The Marseillaise group on the Arc de Triomphe, the Marly horses on the Champs-Elysées, the obelisk in the Place de la Concorde, the Vendôme Column, the sculpture group "La Danse" on the façade of the Opéra, and the Medici Fountain in the Luxembourg Gardens all have been heavily sandbagged. Accordingly, Parisians know what to think of statues and monuments like Rodin's Balzac (NEWSWEEK, July 31, 1939) which are not boxed and boarded up against bombardment.

NEWSWEEK, March 18, 1940

Incompleteness

Adelaide A. Proctor

Nothing resting in its own completeness
Can have worth or beauty; but alone,
Because it leads and tends to further sweetness,
Fuller, higher, deeper than its own.

Spring's real glory dwells not in the meaning,
Gracious though it be, of her blue hours;
But is hidden in her tender leaning
To the summer's richer wealth of flowers.

Dawn is fair because the mists fade slowly
Into day, which floods the world with light.
Twilight's mystery is so sweet and holy,
Just because it ends in starry night.

Childhood's smiles unconscious graces borrow
From strife that in a far-off future lies;
And angel-glances (veiled now by life's sorrow)
Draw our hearts to some beloved eyes.

Life is only bright when it proceedeth
Towards a truer, deeper life above;
Human love is sweetest when it leadeth
To a more divine and perfect love.

Learn the mystery of progression duly;
Do not call each glorious change decay;
But know we only hold our treasures truly
When it seems as if they passed away;

Nor dare to blame God's gifts for incompleteness;
In that want their beauty lies; they roll
Towards some infinite depth of love and sweetness,
Bearing onward man's reluctant soul.

Photo Opposite
SAN XAVIER DEL BAC MISSION
TUCSON, ARIZONA
Fred Sieb Photography

THROUGH MY WINDOW

Pamela Kennedy

The Centurion's Story

It was a hot, dusty day in Jerusalem, and Marcus was in an ill humor. He had been summoned to supervise a crucifixion. This was an unusual duty for a centurion, but Pilate, the Roman governor of occupied Judea, was nervous about this particular crucifixion. Consequently, Marcus, who regularly commanded a company of 100 men, had been ordered to lead the small contingent of soldiers tasked with the execution.

There were three men to be crucified today:

two were thieves and one was a religious zealot of some sort. Apparently Pilate had sentenced this third man because of complaints brought by the Jewish leaders. Marcus cared little about the particulars of the case. His interest was in doing his duty to the satisfaction of his superiors.

As the small party of soldiers and condemned men began the death march to Golgotha, Marcus's attention was riveted upon the one called Jesus. It was obvious the man had been brutalized; beaten with a scourge and seriously injured. He staggered under the weight of the wooden crossbeam he carried, stumbled, and nearly fell. Partly in mercy, but more for expediency, Marcus compelled a bystander to lift the beam and carry it the distance to the hill outside the city gates.

It was at that point Marcus first confronted Jesus face to face, for as the weight was taken from his back, the wounded man straightened and captured the eyes of the centurion with his own. It was a most unsettling look and Marcus quickly turned aside. Pity? Mourning? Grief? The centurion couldn't put a name to it. He had seen many men face death with eyes of anger, hatred, or fear; but none of that was present in this man. Marcus wondered why.

The hill was gained, the men were hung upon the crosses, and Marcus watched with disdain as the soldiers joked and cast lots for the condemned men's cast-off clothes. The centurion stood apart observing the scene as he would a play. He noticed things that had not previously caught his attention. Small groups of women huddled in prayer, weeping silently. Groups of passersby, priests, and city rulers taunted the one called Jesus, challenging him to come down, to prove his claims of diety.

Watching it all, Marcus recalled the stories he had heard over the past three years. Stories of a healer, a teacher, a rabbi who had roamed the countryside speaking about the kingdom of God. He recalled a fellow centurion's story of how this man had healed a dying slave—without ever seeing the man. Marcus remembered now and studied this man called Jesus.

For three long hours he watched. There was no railing at the frenzied crowd or the greedy soldiers, no curses directed at God or man. Instead, to the centurion's surprise, he heard Jesus speak words of forgiveness, of comfort, of encouragement. Almost unconsciously, Marcus moved closer to the cross. Whether it was to hear Jesus's words better or from some other more supernatural compulsion, he didn't know. But in the end, Marcus stood nearly below the crucified man, his eyes captured once again by those of Jesus.

Then the darkness came, chill and black and heavy as a shroud. It was noon, but as dark as midnight—without stars or moon. Still Marcus stood transfixed, outside of time it seemed, staring at the outstretched arms, the lolling head, the bleeding brow.

Finally the wounded head raised, the eyes opened, the chest heaved with the intake of air and a cry shattered the blackness.

"My God, my God! Why hast thou forsaken me?"

Marcus started as Jesus shouted to eternity and brightness pierced the dark. His heart racing, the centurion ordered the soldiers to raise a vinegar-soaked sponge to the condemned man's lips.

"Speak!" Marcus cried, something in him screaming for confirmation of the truth he suspected, for a moment of clear illumination. Was this man truly who he claimed to be? Marcus needed some kind of proof for what his mind and heart were stretching to comprehend.

And then the cry resounded over the bleak hillside, *Tetelestai!*" "It is finished!" It was the victor's cry, shouted by the winner of a race, the one triumphant over his enemies in battle. It was the confirmation Marcus sought!

Falling to his knees before the rugged cross, Marcus heard Jesus speak once more, this time in tones of confidence and peace.

"Father, into thy hands I commend my Spirit."

Marcus watched as the body slumped, lifeless, on the cross. This was no execution, but a confident, deliberate yielding up of life.

As if wrenched in terrestrial grief, the earth beneath Marcus's knees trembled and groaned. Rocks split in deafening cracks. Men and women screamed, ran, and were thrown to the convulsing ground. But for Marcus, fear had passed. He had been lifted by this man called Jesus to a place beyond terror.

His eyes burning with unshed tears, his mind gripping the truth at last, Marcus raised his arms in supplication and praise. There on Golgotha, giving voice to the thunder, the centurion cried out to heaven, "Truly this man was the Son of God!"

Pamela Kennedy is a freelance writer of short stories, articles, essays, and children's books. Married to a naval officer and mother of three children, she has made her home on both U.S. coasts and currently resides in Hawaii. She draws her material from her own experiences and memories, adding bits of imagination to create a story or mood.

The Passion Week Story

Late in the evening he arrived with the twelve. And while they were sitting there, right in the middle of the meal, Jesus remarked, "Believe me, one of you is going to betray me—someone who is now having his supper with me."

This shocked and distressed them and one after another they began to say to him, "Surely, I'm not the one?"

"It is one of the twelve," Jesus told them, "a man who is dipping his hand into the dish with me. It is true that the Son of Man will follow the road foretold by the scriptures, but alas for the man through whom he is betrayed! It would be better for that man if he had never been born."

And while they were still eating Jesus took a loaf, blessed it and broke it and gave it to them, with the words, "Take this, it is my body."

Then he took a cup, and after thanking God, he gave it to them, and they all drank from it, and he said to them: "This is my blood which is shed for many in the new agreement. I tell you truly I will drink no more wine until the day comes when I drink it fresh in the kingdom of God!"

Then they sang a hymn and went out to the Mount of Olives.

Reprinted with permission of Macmillan Publishing Company from THE NEW TESTAMENT MODERN ENGLISH by J. B. Phillips, © 1958, 1960, and 1972 by J. B. Phillips.

Painting opposite
THE LAST SUPPER
by Carl Heinrich Bloch

Then they arrived at a place called Gethsemane, and Jesus said to his disciples, "Sit down here while I pray."

He took with him Peter, James and John, and began to be horror-stricken and desperately depressed. "My heart is nearly breaking," he told them. "Stay here and keep watch for me."

Then he walked forward a little way and flung himself on the ground, praying that, if it were possible, he might not have to face the ordeal. "Dear Father," he said, "all things are possible to you. Please, let me not have to drink this cup! Yet it is not what I want but what you want."

Then he came and found them fast asleep. He spoke to Peter: "Are you asleep, Simon? Couldn't you manage to watch for a single hour? Watch and pray, all of you, that you may not have to face temptation. Your spirit is willing, but human nature is weak."

Then he went away again and prayed in the same words, and once more he came and found them asleep. They could not keep their eyes open and they did not know what to say for themselves.

When he came back for the third time, he said: "Are you still going to sleep and take your ease? All right—the moment has come; now you are going to see the Son of Man betrayed into the hands of evil men! Get up, let us be going! Look, here comes my betrayer!"

Painting opposite
THE AGONY IN THE GARDEN
by Carl Heinrich Bloch

The moment daylight came the chief priests called together a meeting of elders, scribes and members of the whole council, bound Jesus and took him off and handed him over to Pilate. Pilate asked him straight out, "Well, you—are you the king of the Jews?"

"Yes, I am," he replied.

The chief priests brought many accusations. So Pilate questioned him again, "Have you nothing to say? Listen to all their accusations!"

But Jesus made no further answer—to Pilate's astonishment.

Now it was Pilate's custom at festival time to release a prisoner—anyone they asked for. There was in the prison at the time, with some other rioters who had committed murder in a recent outbreak, a man called Barabbas. The crowd surged forward and began to demand that Pilate should do what he usually did for them. So he spoke to them, "Do you want me to set free the king of the Jews for you?"

For he knew perfectly well that the chief priests had handed Jesus over to him through sheer malice. But the chief priests worked upon the crowd to get them to demand Barabbas' release instead. So Pilate addressed them once more, "Then what am I to do with the man whom you call the king of the Jews?"

They shouted back, "Crucify him!"

But Pilate replied, "Why, what crime has he committed?"

But their voices rose to a roar, "Crucify him!"

Painting opposite
PETER'S DENIAL
by Carl Heinrich Bloch

They took him to a place called Golgotha (which means Skull Hill) and they offered him some drugged wine, but he would not take it. Then they crucified him, and shared out his garments, drawing lots to see what each of them would get. It was about nine o'clock in the morning when they nailed him to the cross. Over his head the placard of his crime read, "THE KING OF THE JEWS." They also crucified two bandits at the same time, one on each side of him. And the passers-by jeered at him, shaking their heads in mockery, saying, "Hi, you! You could destroy the Temple and build it up again in three days, why not come down from the cross and save yourself?"

The chief priests also made fun of him among themselves and the scribes, and said: "He saved others, he cannot save himself. If only this Christ, the king of Israel, would come down now from the cross, we should see it and believe!"

And even the men who were crucified with him hurled abuse at him.

At midday darkness spread over the whole countryside and lasted until three o'clock in the afternoon, and at three o'clock Jesus cried out in a loud voice, "My God, my God, why did you forsake me?"

Some of the bystanders heard these words which Jesus spoke in Aramaic (Eloi, Eloi, lama sabachthani?) and said, "Listen, he's calling for Elijah!"

One man ran off and soaked a sponge in vinegar, put it on a stick, and held it up for Jesus to drink, calling out: "Let him alone! Let's see if Elijah will come and take him down!"

But Jesus let out a great cry, and died. The curtain of the Temple sanctuary was split in two from the top to the bottom. And when the centurion who stood in front of Jesus saw how he died, he said, "This man was certainly a son of God!"

Painting opposite
THE CRUCIFIXION
by Carl Heinrich Bloch

When the Sabbath was over, Mary of Magdala, Mary the mother of James, and Salome bought spices so that they could go and anoint him. And very early in the morning on the first day of the week, they came to the tomb, just as the sun was rising.

"Who is going to roll the stone back from the doorway of the tomb?" they asked each other.

And then as they looked closer, they saw that the stone, which was a very large one, had been rolled back. So they went into the tomb and saw a young man in a white robe sitting on the righthand side, and they were simply astonished. But he said to them: "There is no need to be astonished. You are looking for Jesus of Nazareth who was crucified. He has risen; he is not here. Look, here is the place where they laid him. But now go and tell his disciples, and Peter, that he will be in Galilee before you. You will see him there just as he told you."

Painting opposite
THE RESURRECTION
by Carl Heinrich Bloch

Sweet Certainty of Spring

Edith M. Helstern

It's springtime in my garden now—
And memory takes me back
To the little garden on the farm
Down by the woodland tract.

The pear trees growing there, so white,
Bloomed on for many weeks;
And down the winding lane a ways
The apple trees grew pink.

Tall dogwoods, high upon the hill,
Arose like patchy spots of snow;
Green ferns grew nodding by the rill
Where weeping willows grow.

The meadow brook sang softly—
A happy little tune;
And, without fear, a little deer
Drank from the near lagoon.

So, every springtime in my garden
There's music in the air
That takes me back in memory
To the little farm—back there.

Country CHRONICLE

—— Lansing Christman ——

Look at the natural world around you and witness the evidence of God's presence. You will see it in bud and sprout, in bird and bloom, in the newly awakened grass. You will see and hear this presence in running waters flowing down the streams from the spring snowmelt.

We always associate Easter and springtime with the floral beauty of hyacinths and daffodils, lilies and violets, of crocuses and dooryard dandelions. In the woods we eagerly seek those secluded spots where the first trailing arbutus comes into bloom. And we associate all these with the renewal of life. Every shoot, blossom, and tendril reminds us of the resurrection of life as told in the story of Easter.

There are also pleasing reminders of the renewal of life to be found in the bird world. Listen to the chorus at dawn. It is a song of spring, as if all of nature is taking a role in the celebration of Easter. You will hear the warble of the bluebird, the carol of the robin, the dove's "coo," the whistle of cardinals and meadowlarks. As the day's

sun warms, you will see the birds inspecting old nesting sites in shady trees and cubbyholes on behalf of the young to come.

Look at the goldfinches: the males are going through their changing of the guard, and their plumage is transformed from dull olive to brilliant hues of gold and vivid dark wings. Theirs is a hue that glows from within, like the night sky changing to day as darkness is given over to the sunrise.

We let the dandelions grow. They dot the grass with golden gems. They go to seed and the goldfinches come to feed on the parachute-like fibers that the wind carries—the seeds of the dandelion—to bring new life somewhere in the countryside.

At this Eastertime, line your heart with fiber as soft and fine as these seeds of the dandelion, with the fluff of thistledown, or with the dander of the cattails in the marsh. Line it with the sweetness of the goldfinches' song.

Then you will understand the sense of Easter and the Resurrection, when our hearts and souls can put aside unhappiness and receive the pure message of God's love for us all. As spring begins, Easter places at your fingertips a whole new universe of eternal life.

The author of two published books, Lansing Christman has been contributing to Ideals for almost twenty years. Mr. Christman has also been published in several American, foreign, and braille anthologies. He and his wife, Lucile, live in rural South Carolina where they enjoy the pleasures of the land around them.

Kindness to Animals

Author Unknown

Little children, never give
Pain to things that feel and live;
Let the gentle robin come
For the crumbs you save at home.
As his meat you throw along,
He'll repay you with a song;
Never hurt the timid hare
Peeping from her green grass lair—
Let her come and sport and play
On the lawn at close of day;
The little lark goes soaring high
To the bright windows of the sky,
Singing as if 'twere always spring,
And fluttering on an untired wing—
Oh! Let him sing his happy song
Nor do these gentle creatures wrong.

Photo Opposite
WHITE RABBIT AND DANDELIONS
Bob Firth/Firth Photobank

BITS & PIECES

You go forth into the world at a time when the rushing current of modern life threatens to take every man from his feet, whose feet do not stand upon duty, and whose hands are not stretched forth toward God.

Noah Porter

The greatest homage we can pay to truth is to use it.

Ralph Waldo Emerson

If you would imitate Christ, take sin by the throat and the sinner by the hand.

W. H. H. Murray

Truth is tough; it will not break like a bubble at a touch; nay, you may kick it about all day like a football and it will be round and full at evening.

Oliver Wendell Holmes

The triumphs of truth are the most glorious, chiefly because they are the most bloodless of all victories, deriving their highest lustre from the number of the saved, not of the slain.

C. C. Colton

Our thoughts are the epochs in our lives; all else is but as a journal of the winds that blew while we were here.

Henry Thoreau

Let fate do her worst,
    there are relics of joy,
Bright dreams of the past,
    which she cannot destroy,
That come in the nighttime
    of sorrow and care
And bring back the features
    that joy used to wear.

Long, long be my heart
    with such memories filled,
Like the vase in which roses
    have once been distilled;
You may break, you may shatter
    the vase if you will
But the scent of the roses
    will hang around still.

Thomas Moore

Lord! we would put aside
The gauds and baubles of this mortal life—
Weak self-conceit, the foolish tools of strife,
    The tawdry garb of pride—
    And pray, in Christ's dear name,
Thy grace to deck us in the robes of light;
That at His coming we may stand aright
    And fear no sudden shame.

An Advent Carol

Let us beware of losing our enthusiasms. Let us ever glory in something and strive to retain our admiration for all that would ennoble and our interest in all that would enrich and beautify our life.

Phillips Brooks

Right forever on the scaffold;
    wrong on the throne;
But the scaffold sways the future,
    and behind the dim unknown
Standeth God within the shadow,
    keeping watch above his own.

James Russell Lowell

Gethsemane

All those who journey, soon or late,
Must pass within the garden gate;
Must kneel alone in darkness there,
And battle with some fierce despair.
God pity those who cannot say:
"Not mine but thine;" who only pray:
"Let this cup pass," and cannot see
The purpose in Gethsemane.

Ella Wheeler Wilcox

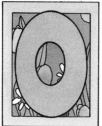n Easter Day
we go to church.
I love to smell the flowers
and hear the songs.

But the best part is to know
that you are still alive, Jesus,
and to remember
that you love even me.

We love because he first loved us.

1 John 4:19

All Gardeners Kneel

Edna Jaques

All gardeners kneel to do their work—
   Sowing a garden, planting shrubs,
Or weeding out a tiny patch
   Where rhubarb shows its little nubs.
We must get close to Mother Earth,
   Feel her glowing like a hearth.

For underneath the quiet ground
   There is a rhythm and a beat—
Life answering to other life
   Below the barley and the wheat.
The clover and the grasses know
   The forces hidden far below.

The cattle on the distant hill
   Lie down beneath the purple skies,
Resting upon the ancient earth.
   But cattle too must kneel to rise,
And sheep close by the river's brink
   Oft lean upon their knees to drink.

So gardeners kneel in the warm sun
   To sow the seeds of fruit and flower
Or tamp a tiny seedling in,
   Part of the lovely springtime hour
When all Creation seems to feel
   A blessed urge to stop and kneel.

CRAFTWORKS

Easter Wreath

Family members and guests who approach your front door will find a festive greeting in the fragrance and eye appeal of this beautiful and easy-to-make Easter wreath. The secret ingredient is the potpourri which fills the bird's nest and is hidden behind the flowers in tiny mesh bags. The materials needed for making this wreath are readily available in craft stores.

Add a whiff of springtime to your door!

Materials Needed:

One 24-inch grapevine wreath
Hot glue gun (recommended for fast drying)
Silk or imitation silk flowers:
Six long sprigs of forsythia
Four medium-size sprigs of lilac
Six large daffodils
Five medium-size jonquils
Four large purple irises
Small nest and bird
Potpourri
Six 3- to 4-inch squares of tulle for potpourri bags
Thin wire for attaching bags to back of wreath, cut in six 6-inch lengths
Six small plastic bird eggs
White glue

Step One: Attaching Flowers

Begin with the forsythia: twine stems into wreath, using photograph as model. Spot glue lower stems to wreath with hot glue gun. When glue has dried, twine stems of lilacs into wreath so that flowers face outward, and spot glue with glue gun.

Remove the daffodil, jonquil, and iris flowers from their stems. Choose three or four of the leaves on the discarded stems and glue in place, then glue the flowers in place by their plastic bases, facing some towards the inside of the wreath and some toward the outside. Draw the lilac leaves forward as you situate the daffodils and jonquils so that leaves surround flowers gracefully.

Step Two: Attaching the Nest

The nest is attached to the wreath as are the flowers, with the glue gun. Proceed likewise to secure the bird at nest edge.

Step Three: Adding Potpourri

Place a pinch of potpourri in the center of each tulle square, draw edges up to make a sack, and secure with fine wire. Working from the back, attach the sacks behind the flowers by twining the ends of the wire ties into the vine.

Turning the wreath to the front, place upright in hanging position and fill nest with loose potpourri. Place the small bird's eggs on top of the filling, using white glue to secure in place.

Joan Alberstadt

Joan Alberstadt is a former commercial artist whose sewing and crafts are available through her business, The Cat's Meow. She enjoys making gifts for her family and friends to brighten up spirits and keep the world looking fresh. She makes her Easter wreaths in Nashville, Tennessee.

Photo Opposite
Gerald Koser

FROM MY G·A·R·D·E·N JOURNAL

Deana Deck

The Legendary Dogwood

The flowering dogwoods are my favorite harbingers of spring. You can trust them not to fool you. Unlike the crocus, which will pop up on Groundhog Day when we all know more winter is ahead, or the foolish robin who often stays in the neighborhood all winter, the dogwood bides its time. When it blooms you can rest easy, knowing that summer is just down the path. I don't plant seeds or set out young plants until the dogwoods are in full bloom.

There is a clean look to a blooming dogwood that appeals to me, especially when glimpsed in the wild, massed against the dark green of pines or mountain laurel. It seems to purify the landscape, making it ready for the growth of a new season.

This purity of appearance adds credibility to its legend. At the time of the crucifixion of Christ, so the tale is told, the dogwood was tall and straight, the size of oaks and elms. So strong was its wood that it was selected to be used for timber to build the cross. The tree was appalled to be put to such use. Jesus, sensing its distress, promised that nevermore should the dogwood grow large enough to be used as a cross. He also promised to create for the dogwood a reminder of his death in the form of the flower: four blossoms shaped in the form of a white cross, with a stain at the outer edge of each petal, and in the center a tiny crown of thorns.

Today the little dogwood faithfully blooms at Eastertime, relaying to us an ancient reminder of the cycle of winter and spring, death and rebirth.

That the dogwood's wood is dense and hard is no legend. It has historically been used for heads of golf clubs and for shuttles in knitting machines. It has also been a favored wood for splitting logs and for skewering meat for roasting on an open fire since it did not burn quickly. The name dogwood, in fact, is thought by some to be a corruption of "dagwood," a Scandinavian word meaning meat skewer.

Others say the name was derived from the fact that the bark, when boiled in water, formed a useful solution for washing dogs suffering from mange. This is not the only medicinal use to which the plant has been put: long before the discovery of quinine, dogwood was one of the many barks used to treat high fevers.

Although the classic dogwood is the pristine white variety found in the wild, today's nurseries have bred lovely pale pink ones and others are available with rich ruby-red blooms. Another development is that of a tree with variegated leaves. The Cherokee Sunset, for example, offers bright green and yellow summer foliage that turns shades of pink, purple, and red in fall. The Cherokee Daybreak variety features green leaves edged with creamy white. This gives way in fall to pink and deep red. The dogwoods all wind up the season with a brilliant display of red berries, to the joy of the birds. Thirty-six species of birds are known to seek out the dogwood berry.

Cornus florida, the common flowering dogwood seen most often, is native to zone five. It doesn't flourish in the extreme north, but the New Hampshire dogwood does well in zone four climates. The New Hampshire dogwood, on the other hand, cannot survive hot southern summers.

The key to success in growing dogwoods is knowledge of their native habitat. They are what is known as an understory tree. That means they grow under the protecting shelter of larger trees. Seldom are they in direct sunlight in summer, but in soft, filtered shade. In early spring, just prior to blooming, they benefit from the full sunlight that streams through the still-bare branches of the taller trees.

In order to provide your dogwood with the balance between sunlight and shade which it would have chosen in a forest, be sure to choose a location which is partially shaded during the hot summer months, bearing in mind that the soil should be slightly acidic as are the heavily mulched forest floors where dogwoods are found growing wild. Dig a hole slightly larger than the root ball of your specimen, add mulch to the hole before planting, and water thoroughly.

The dogwood's delicate fleshy root system grows near the soil surface, making it vulnerable to drought. The greatest cause of failure of newly planted trees is the lack of adequate moisture. A new tree should be watered thoroughly once a week for the first summer after planting. Moist roots, filtered shade, and cool soil conditions keep a dogwood thriving.

The trees are not heavy feeders. In fact, excessive fertilization can actually damage the roots. Fertilizing will not be necessary until your new tree is at least two years old, and then avoid high nitrogen mixtures; you will sacrifice blooms for foliage. A 5-10-10 mixture is preferred, but use it sparingly and keep it away from the trunk.

Mulching is a good way to provide nutrients to the soil around the dogwood while conserving moisture and keeping the delicate roots cool in summer.

Don't be alarmed if your dogwood doesn't produce the same amount of blooms each year. It is not uncommon for one to bloom profusely, set a bumper crop of berries, and then bloom poorly the next year. It has simply used up all its energy and is taking a season off to recuperate. Something we all need to do occasionally.

Deana Deck is a frequent contributor to Nashville *magazine, and her garden column is a regular feature in the* Tennessean. *Ms. Deck grows her dogwoods in Nashville, Tennessee.*

RUN-AWAY

Helen Virden

A river is a stay-at-home
Banked in by willow trees.
It is satisfied to move
Tranquilly, at ease.

But mountain streams romp over rocks,
Rush through tangled vines,
Or cascade from a mountain top,
Clear as sparkling wines.

A river hugs a gentle hill,
Content to stay at home;
But mountain streams are run-aways
Of crashing, spilling foam.

Photo Opposite
LILIUOKALANI GARDEN PARK
OAHU, HAWAII
Ed Cooper Photography

CAPTIVATING COVES

Early spring is a special time at the Great Smoky Mountains National Park. Last year's leaves still crunch underfoot; the air is brisk, clean, and sweet; the trees are bare except for the early bud-poppers in the lowlands, and the delicate new flowers—the bloodroots and the wild ginger, hint at what is in store as the vernal equinox advances. The streets of Cherokee, North Carolina, and of towns across the mountains in Tennessee are nearly free of tourists; the shopkeepers lounge, free of care; and the wild doves drift off, two by two, into the landscape. There is a sense of timelessness.

It is a fine time to be just drifting like the doves. A sense of impending discovery leads one away from the ordinary—the artificial cloisters of the towns, the domesticity of daffodils blooming dutifully among the headstones at the local church—to hiking trails which lead to a world of giants, untouched trees in cove forests.

The Smokies are not as they were a hundred years ago. Gone are the giant trees which once covered every cove, hill, and valley. They are metamorphosed now into shingles and railroad ties, paper and ax handles. Yet there remains a tantalizing suspicion that not all of that old world could have vanished without a trace.

In fact, pristine cove forests—deeply recessed, low-lying coves on the northeastern side of the Smokies—have survived, perhaps due to their inaccessibility. They continue to elude visitors even though their positions are clearly marked on the maps at the Sugarlands visitor center. But once embarked upon, easy hiking trails coax the spring drifter back into what appears to be a different geological era when trees grew to giant

TOWERING TREES AND SUNLIGHT
SMOKY MOUNTAINS NATIONAL PARK
GATLINBURG, TENNESSEE
Adam Jones

proportions.

Wide, nearly level trails are made pleasant enough by rhododendron, mountain laurel, ferns, the lichen-gray boles of tulip poplars, and young, muscular beeches. Along each wide trail one sees familiar species of arrow-straight trees such as sugar and red maples, silver bells, tulip poplars, and two kinds of magnolias. The Smokies have hundreds of such walking places. But as the trail enters a cove, everything is out of proportion—enormous and ancient.

Silver bells, which are known to be spindly shrubs and small trees in other parts of the mountains, are huge things with purplish, flaking bark; and the maples are enormous, both in girth and in height, holding their leaves so far above the ground that binoculars are required for recognition. On the forest floor are great limbs, some of them larger around than whole tree trunks in the outside world. They molder and gradually return to the soil which nurtured them. Hemlocks, beeches, and tulip poplars, their first limbs a hun-

dred feet up, their trunks many feet around, astound the dwarfed observer. The wind gives the standing giants elegantly ponderous movement, and the power of that gentle motion is felt by the earth below.

Nearly all of these patriarchs have been decapitated. Lightning has sought out the tallest spars in the forest and has sent their crowns crashing back to the floor. On a mountaintop it is a liability to be too tall. But that too is part of the centuries-long development of a prehistoric forest.

In the spring, a time of fresh beginnings, it is inspiring to visit a world which seems to know no end.

Branley Allan Branson

Branley Allan Branson is Professor of Biology at Eastern Kentucky University. He has published hundreds of articles about nature, travel, and natural history in over 180 publications. He lives with his wife, a photographer and writer, in Richmond, Kentucky.

Coronation Pavilion*

Honolulu's Iolani Palace

A little before noon each Friday, when the Hawaiian sun is at its highest, a small crowd gathers on the lawn of Iolani Palace. In the crowd are visitors from all over the world who come to see the only royal palace under the American flag. Some, brown paper lunch bags in hand, are office workers from the shining skyscrapers of nearby downtown Honolulu. A few set up folding chairs under trees gently ruffled by trade winds.

The crowd is dotted with bits of color. Many wear leis of flowers, *ohia lehua*, fiery red and sacred to Pele, Mother of volcanoes and *pandanus*, yellow as the *Palila* bird of the forest.

To those who understand the language of the flowers, each blossom sends forth a message. A young mother wears a lei of *loke-lani*, delicate pink roses, and smiling Hawaiians offer best wishes for her child who has just been christened, perhaps at Kawaiaha'o church across the street.

On the lawn not far away, another woman wears garlands of *pikake*, the island relative of jasmine, which scent the breeze with their jasmine fragrance. Newlywed, she smiles shyly at the man sitting next to her. Her mother and her grandmother, as is the Hawaiian tradition, wore *pikake* when they were brides.

The people sit around a large ornate bandstand. Once a king was crowned here—Kalakaua, by the grace of God and the will of the people, ruler of all Hawaii. That was in 1883, when lily pads still floated on the ponds of Waikiki and there were grass houses at Waimanalo.

It is appropriate that Kalakaua's coronation pavilion serve as a bandstand, for he was a man who deeply loved the music of Hawaii. It was Kalakaua, called by some the "Merry Monarch," who decreed that the ancient chants silenced by the missionaries be freely heard in the islands and that the hula be danced again.

As the crowd makes itself comfortable, several musicians mount the bandstand. At twelve sharp the conductor raises his baton and the Royal Hawaiian Band offers its first selection.

The first music played by the band will be, as always, "Hawaii Ponoi." The people come to their feet and stand until the music is finished. It is the official state song. Once it was the anthem of the kingdom.

Before the concert is over there will be a few popular tunes and a couple of marches. There will also be one or two hulas, the dancers moving gracefully on the lawn. One might be a classical *mele* hula danced to the click of the *'ili'ili* stones and the *ipu* gourd drum. The other may be a more modern interpretation. The hula, like all arts, is a constantly evolving dance.

The last music played by the band will be, as always, "Aloha Oe." The song, with its haunting words of farewell, was written by King Kalakaua's sister. Her name was Lili'uokalani and she was every inch a queen.

Queen Lili'uokalani succeeded her brother Kalakaua after his death in 1891, but she was destined to be the last Hawaiian monarch.

In January 1893 the throne of Hawaii fell in revolution. A counterrevolution followed two years later, a movement swiftly crushed, in which Lili'uokalani played no part. She was made a prisoner in what had once been her palace. In the throne room of the Iolani Palace,

Throne Room*

Queen Lili'uokalani was pronounced "guilty of treason" and placed under house arrest for nearly a year.

Lili'uokalani lived on until 1917 in her home on Bertania Street. From her window she could see the walls of Iolani Palace.

The government of Hawaii went through

Iolani Palace, Oahu Hawaii*

Queen Liliuokalani seated on chair in Iolani Palace, circa 1890

many changes until statehood was ratified by Congress in 1959. The Iolani Palace weathered the course of Hawaiian history and served as the capitol building of the Republic, the Territory, and eventually the state of Hawaii, until in 1969 the state moved its offices into a splendid new building and turned the palace over to the Friends of the Iolani Palace. Restoration began at once, a long, painstaking process that still continues.

Weary with years, the old building sagged two inches forward. Termites had ravaged the walls and the ornate iron work was coated with rust. The palace was fumigated and the rust and peeling paint sandblasted away. Reinforcing steel beams replaced aging wood.

But in the years after the revolution, the possessions of the royal household were scattered across the world. Much is still missing and may never be found. Still, the search continues. Some artifacts of the monarchy are displayed in Oahu's Bishop Museum and are part of the world's foremost collection of Hawaiian and Polynesian antiquities.

Antiques from the monarchy were returned by families who had treasured them since the revolution. Silver flatware, a gift from France's Napoleon I to King Kamehameha IV; a glis-

Statue of Queen Lili'uokalani

tening Bohemian crystal decanter used by Kalakaua; damask napkins; a pearl-handled knife; and creamy stationary embossed with the royal coat-of-arms.

Today the Iolani Palace is once again a showcase of Hawaiian culture and history and is open to the public. The magnificent *koa* wood central staircase gleams in the soft light of frosted glass doors. In the throne room red velvet drapes hang again from windows decorated with carved golden crowns. Fine china is set out for a state dinner in the formal dining room. There are fresh flowers in the queen's bedroom and papers await the royal signature in the library. The presence of Lili'uokalani can be felt once again.

In the Nu'uanu Valley where the mist comes down from the Ko'olau Mountains are the royal tombs where Lili'uokalani is buried. A visitor has placed a lei of *pikake* flowers, which she loved, in front of her tomb. The cold marble is warmed with the fragrance of jasmine.

Michael McKeever is a Contributing Editor of Country Inns *magazine and a frequent contributor to* Physicians Travel. *At journey's end, Michael enjoys returning home to Imperial Beach, California.*

Easter

Jesus, our Redeemer, arose on Easter morn,
Thus fulfilled the purpose for which He had been born.
In anguish in the garden, all our sins He bore,
Suffered on the cross that we might live forevermore.
His love, unequaled, transcends all we know on earth.
He died that we might partake of that great Rebirth.
How can we thank Him for this in our own small way?
What we do for others is for Him, the scriptures say.

June C. Bush
Rexburg, Idaho

Spring Shower

The soft sprinkling sounds of a shower,
That first hypnotic spring rain,
Enchant the heart and lift the spirit,
Soul refreshed from the refrain.

An invitation to bear witness
And sit in still repose,
Relax and welcome the performance
As nature changes clothes.

Emerald arrangements are everywhere,
Buds and blossoms swell and nod,
Bees and butterflies abound in boughs,
Blushed with hope and blessed by God.

Barbara Genettie
New Tripoli, Pennsylvania

Reflections

Sowing and Reaping

I want a garden wondrous, fair,
So I'll sow seeds with loving care.
I'll plant and weed and cultivate;
Sun and rain will participate,
Bringing my garden in beauty to bloom
Where birds will sing their springtime tune,
And bees, searching pollen, will softly hum,
And bright butterflies to the flowers will come
Reaping all this beauty. I want to share
The miracle of my garden fair.
For sharing is thanks to God above
And doubles our joy when we give with love.

Louise Taylor Tucker
Erie, Pennsylvania

Editor's Note: Readers are invited to submit
unpublished, original poetry, short anecdotes,
and humorous reflections on life for possible
publication in future *Ideals* issues. Please send
copies only; manuscripts will not be returned.
Writers receive $10 for each published
submission. Send material to "Readers'
Reflections," Ideals Publishing Corporation,
P.O. Box 140300, Nashville, Tennessee 37214-
0300.

First Love

I was hurrying to work
When he whistled at me.
I stopped in my tracks
And turned round to see
Him standing there waiting,
Not saying a thing.
And right then I loved that
First robin of spring!

Ardis Rittenhouse
Alexandria, Indiana

A SLICE OF LIFE

Edgar A. Guest

The rich may pay for orchids rare but, Oh, the apple tree
Flings out its blossoms to the world for every eye to see,
And all who sigh for loveliness may walk beneath the sky
And claim a richer beauty than man's gold can ever buy.

The blooming cherry trees are free for all to look upon;
The dogwood buds for all of us, and not some favorite one;
The wide outdoors is no man's own; the stranger on the street
Can cast his eyes on many a rose and claim its fragrance sweet.

Small gardens are shut in by walls, but none can wall the sky,
And none can hide the friendly trees from all who travel by;
And none can hold the apple boughs and claim them for his own,
For all the beauties of the earth belong to God alone.

So let me walk the world just now and wander far and near;
Earth's loveliness is mine to see; its music mine to hear;
There's not a single apple bough that spills its blooms about
But I can claim the joy of it, and none can shut me out.

Edgar A. Guest began his illustrious career in 1895 at the age of fourteen when his work appeared in the Detroit Free Press. *His column was syndicated in over 300 newspapers, and he became known as "The Poet of the People." Mr. Guest captured the hearts of vast radio audiences with his weekly program, "It Can Be Done" and, until his death in 1959, published many treasured volumes of poetry.*

A Prayer for Dawn

Douglas Malloch

We pray before we go to bed;
I wish we prayed at morn instead,
Or night and morn. Although we need
Confess tonight today's misdeed,
When in the morning light we rise
We need new faith to face new skies.

So I would write a pray'r for dawn:
O Father, when the night is gone,
Its sins forgiven, washed away,
Give me the strength to live today.
Now standing in the new day's light,
Give me the strength to live it right.

When I arise from gentle sleep,
I have a little house to keep.
God guard my tongue and guard my mind
And help me keep them clean and kind.
Through life's temptations, anger, hate,
Help me this day to travel straight.

I am not looking down the years;
A nearer duty now appears.
For years are, after all, the sum
Of our todays that daily come.
The morn is here. O Lord, I pray,
Give me the strength to live today.

Readers' Forum

I was given my first Ideals *by my grandmother. I truly enjoyed it then and I appreciate it more and more every day. I flip through my* Ideals *often and always feel a sense of warmth and love. The poems, short articles, and pictures always make me feel wonderful. I love wandering through antique shops and finding your magazines. I'm like a child in a candy store. Thank you for making such a beautiful magazine.*

Tina G. Augustus
Del Valle, Texas

My wife and I are so engrossed in your books that they take us back to those wonderful family childhood memories, into some very special moments in time in our lives. Reading Ideals *is inspirational and surely makes every yesterday a dream of happiness and every tomorrow a vision of hope.*

Robert E. Agan
Westfield, Massachusetts

We're a homeschool family and use Ideals *for poetry. It is especially enjoyable to have each issue draw us into the celebration of each changing season or holiday. Some days we pick a beautiful photograph and each take a turn sharing what we would be doing if we were actually there. For all the family times you have made so special, we again say thanks.*

The Hamann Family
Judy, Drew, Jennifer, and Nathanael
Toledo, Ohio

Want to share your crafts?
Readers are invited to submit original craft ideas for possible development and publication in future Ideals *issues. Please send query letter (with photograph, if possible) to Editorial Features Department, Ideals Publishing Corporation, P.O. Box 140300, Nashville, Tennessee 37214-0300. Please do not send craft samples; they cannot be returned.*

ideals
Celebrating Life's Most Treasured Moments

Photo Opposite
QUIET STREAM
Donald Mills